Chapter 1

Meet Swamp Hattie

Spanish moss hair covered head and pits.
Feed bags and burlap shrouded shoulders and
  hips.
A black-water pearl replaced one eye
On a face that made even the Devil cry:
Swamp muck skin, scarred and pocked;
Cauliflower ears exposed through her locks;
An aardvark nose smashed to one side;
Oozing sores and boils trapped maggots that
  died;
Coarse, kinky hair stubbled her chin;
Thick crusted lips showed where warts had
  been
Nibbled away by decaying, cratered teeth,
Four on top and three beneath;
A tongue so wicked it was scaled and forked
Lurked inside her mouth, all cocked and
  torqued.
Her hands were gnarled like cypress tree roots
With fingernail beds like the beaks of black
  coots
That cut like sabers and were covered with
  soot,
Topping long, curved fingers of at least a foot.
What the burlap hid, only God knew for sure:
Suffice it to say, it was dark, gross, impure.

Her breath stank of putrid meals:
Cow patties for breakfast; moccasins for
   lunch;
Rotten fish for supper; road kill for brunch.
Slimes and molds: her vegetables du jour;
The fungus she licked grew on manure.
Swamp-water cocktails and pureed turtle
   youths
Washed it all down where it boiled in her juice.
Alligators cringed at even the thought
Of the gasses she passed and the smells she
   brought.

She slithered the swamps looking for meat:
Any thing to beat;
Any thing to eat.
Always on attack; never in retreat.
With hatred and anger her actions replete:
A relentless renegade that never slept,
A heartless spirit that never wept.
She gains no relief from the fate she mulls:
Ancient memories that echo through her skull.

Chapter 2

Hattie and the Sailor

Born a princess, pretty and pristine,
To the social elite of St. Augustine,
Beautiful, intelligent, wealthy and more,
The envy of all -- whom she ignored.
The mirror contained what she adored:
Statuesque Hattie with a rotten core.
Family and friends, they mattered not,
Nor did any of the living lot.
She had everything that money bought;
She had it all, or so she thought.
Then one day a galleon brought
A dashing young man every woman sought
Who glanced her way and instantly caught
The fever for feelings he had forever fought.
She returned his stare and became acutely
  aware
That her heart pounded -- how could it dare!
She refused to believe she could possibly care
For the dark tanned sailor who continued to
  stare.

Oh, how she changed right from the start!
He loved her so much! How he played the part,
Until he unleashed his poisonous dart
That left her alone and pierced her heart.
Her ruptured soul hemorrhaged outside and
   in,
Drowning all life, deadening her skin;
Killing human traits that arise within;
Creating pure hatred for women and for men.
Fleeing those feelings she no longer felt,
Rejecting the cards in the hand she was dealt,
Forging a memory that would never melt,
She fashioned a noose from his favorite belt.

Chapter 3

Hattie, Heaven, and Hell

Rejected by Heaven for her hate of mankind;
Express shipped to Hades, one of Lucifer's
    finds;
Her evil doubled, then tripled, then
    quadrupled again,
And Satan himself feared the evil within.
Afraid of her anger and scared by her hate,
Satan exiled his creation and sealed-up her
    fate:
"Return to the house where you gave up your
    life;
Suffer forever in agony and strife!"
Rejected by all and confined to her home,
Her wickedness grew, as she stewed alone,
And replaced her beauty with blood, guts, and
    gore,
Which erupted from every orifice and pore.

Chapter 4

Terror for the Ancient City

Her powers enormous, she had learned from
  the best;
She escaped from her prison and took up the
  quest
To recruit evil spirits from the East and the
  West
To haunt the Ancient City: create fear and
  unrest.
All went well from the very first,
As the terror and destruction quenched her
  thirst.
The more evil she did, the more ugly she grew
Until the last of her dwindling, marauding
  crew
Cried, "Enough is enough; that's all we'll do!"
She continued alone with her despicable ways,
Haunting the nights and even the days,
Scaring and pillaging and destroying the
  peace:
Spreading disease and destruction and
  contaminating the feast.
A hurricane she summoned with winds never
  to cease.
Her grip on the town's throat she refused to
  release.
Panicked and frightened and fleeing for life,
The citizens demanded an end to the strife.

But their pleas just added fuel to the fire:
Her bitterness and hate would never expire.

Chapter 5

The Minorcan Witch

So the governor consulted a Minorcan witch
Who laughed at their plight with this ghostly
  bitch
Until she saw Hattie in her crystal ball:
Such grotesqueness she could never, ever
  recall.
Immediately sensing the danger to all,
She agreed to help, to answer this call.
A potion she poured into the bay,
And it arose with the fog into the clouds some
  way,
Causing all spirits in the city in unison to say:
"Hattie's time has come; she must go away.
Expel her forever, away from our coast;
She's too ghastly and gross, even for ghosts."

Chapter 6

Massacre at the Old Fort

Merging witch magic and ghostly powers,
Three hundred spirits at the midnight hour
Left their haunted homes and ships in port,
Assembled downtown in front of the fort,
Gathered their weapons, donned their gear,
And confronted the demon that they too
   feared.
The titans clashed as the typhoon roared;
Even God and Satan could not ignore
The quaking earth and thunderous doom;
The hideous horrors cast from her womb;
The killing and maiming of spiritual beings,
Crushed, defeated and now rapidly fleeing
The wrath and ugliness of Ms. Hattie.

Chapter 7

Swamp Hattie
Wins Her Kingdom

Seeing the battle was clearly lost
And wanting to end this at any cost,
God and the Devil demanded a truce,
Parted the storm, and played their deuce:
"Hattie, you've won, but here's your deal.
This is it; you cannot appeal."
From Twelve Mile Swamp to just east of the
   river
All the wetlands and beasts they decided to
   give her.
"Here you'll stay until Judgment Day
When I will implode and do away
With this globe and the evil that exists,
And you, my Hattie, are first on the list."

God also decreed,
And the Devil agreed:
"This blackwater kingdom you shall never
   leave,
From this sentence there is no reprieve.
The creatures there are yours to use,
Torture, dissect, kill, or abuse.
We will pity their souls when their time is
   done,
Remembering well their living Hell where you
   had your fun.
We fear for the people who cross your path.

We know they'll see and feel your wrath.
To protect mankind from your hideous larks,
We'll make the swamp foreboding, damp, and
   dark.
I'll give you an eye for all to see;
Even in darkness, a warning to flee.
I'll give you a stench for all to smell,
So even the children will run and tell.
I'll even finish the look that fits you so well:
Grotesqueness far greater than
   the ugliness of Hell."

Chapter 8

Swamp Hattie's Warning

Hearing her sentence she made one last stand;
Steaming and huffing she gave one final
  command:

"Venture not into my swamp!
No god, no creature, no man!"

Chapter 9

Swamp Hattie's Domain

So Swamp Hattie was born that day in July,
A day God, Satan, and the angels all cried;
A day the spirits and souls of St. Augustine
    sighed;
The day the hopes of all swamp creatures died.
Even to this day Swamp Hattie still roams
From US 1 to King and Bear homes,
From the St. Johns' banks through Turnbull
    Creek.
Not a year, not a month nor even a week
Goes by without someone hearing her shriek.
From her containment she occasionally sneaks
To steal a calf, a cow, or even a horse,
Consuming it all as a snack or main course.
And all the year, not just on Halloween,
Beware as you travel on State Road 16
Because Hattie does lurk in the ditches unseen
To abduct and devour a child or a teen.
But all are at risk from this demon queen
Of ghouls and goblins and things in between.

Now everyone living near Hattie's domain
Locks windows and doors and inside remains
Every day of the year when the daylight wanes.
And fishermen dare not in the creeks be found
When the sun sets and the light lowers down.
And golfers, too, abandon their balls

That slice or hook where dense shadows
    sprawl.
For Swamp Hattie waits there for the short and
    tall,
Waiting in winter, summer, spring, and fall.
And Cracker cowboys croon late after noon
While hugging their campfires and avoiding
    the moon,
For the light of the dawn simply can't come too
    soon.
And never do they rope, wrangle, or ride
Near the palmetto edges where Swamp Hattie
    hides.
And four wheel mudders find other
    playgrounds
Than the mucks and bogs where Hattie gowns.
And coon hunters tremble
As they gather and assemble
To track their howling hounds
Into the bush where Hattie's found.
And how quickly they abandon their
    challenging chase
When their four-legged quarry enters Hattie's
    hiding place.

And all those swamp sounds you hear every
   night?

The croaking of frogs?
The squealing of hogs?
The screeching of owls?
The barks of wild dogs?
The howls of coyotes?
The whistling of ducks?
The grunts of gators?
The snorting of bucks?
The hissing of snakes?
The whippoorwills' call?

Are the voices of Swamp Hattie
   beckoning to all!

Epilogue

Take care where you travel near this City of
   Old.
Does Swamp Hattie still live here? Is she still
   strong and bold?
You've heard she's dead, or so you've been told;
Such rumors run rampant --
   they're uncontrolled.
Best you remember that eye and that stench:
They warn you of danger from this ghostly
   wench.
Protect yourself and especially your friends;
Don't let them tell you she's only "pretend."
Take frequent rear and side view glances;
Don't take any unnecessary chances.
Is she alive or is she gone?
You cannot afford to guess wrong
Or you'll likely join that large throng
Who failed to survive
And were eaten alive
By the legend known as…

Swamp Hattie!

The End

Book 1

The Return of
Swamp Hattie

Book 2 of the Swamp Hattie Trilogy

Prologue

Years, days, and even centuries passed,
And Swamp Hattie haunted the first and the
    last,
Plotting and planning and pursuing her prey,
Mostly at night, just as deadly in day.
She pushed the boundaries that God had made
And trespassed onto properties that He had
    forbade.
Biding her time while plotting her crimes,
She subdued her anger and returned to her
    prime,
More powerful and dangerous and subtly evil:
The most treacherous force since time
    primeval.

Chapter 1

Swamp Hattie's History

When God banished Hattie to her swamp
    habitat,
She showed no mercy to anything: not cats,
    not rats, not even the gnats!
Exiled to the swamps of the St. Johns River--
The only kingdom God would give her--
She continued to kill, massacre, and maim,
Terrorizing all as one and the same.
Soon nothing was left to torture or tame.
So slowly, but surely, she tired of her game.
Then rarely leaving to haunt or roam,
She merged with the muck that was her home.
Her body shriveled, just skin and bones
    remained.
Only a wisp of her powers she retained.
Just as God planned, the end to her reign.
Swamp Hattie was forgotten; our fear faded
    fast--
A mere ghost of a memory-- a nightmare past.
All thought she was gone,
But how they were wrong!

The signs of Swamp Hattie gradually returned.
Small things at first, like a church that burned,
Or a supposed suicide with a mass murder,
Or a worker crushed by a collapsing steel
    girder,

Or the naked skeletal bones found in a shallow
   grave,
Or the drowned scuba divers in Jenny's crystal
   caves,
Or all those missing children and Amber
   Alerts,
Or the multitudes of auto accidents that
   injured, maimed, and hurt.
All these were signs, more subtle it's true.
There they were, clue upon clue:
Messages to me and signs to you.
Hattie had learned new lessons; give her her
   due.
By learning new ways, Swamp Hattie was
   reborn:
From a ghoul that haunted and taunted even
   the newborn
To a silent, undercover terrorist, she was
   transformed.

How did this happen, when even God thought
   she was done?
How did this happen, when even God thought
   He'd won?
What could possibly occur to renew Hattie's
   run
Of death, destruction, and her despicable fun?

Chapter 2

Swamp Hattie Awakens!

Swamp Hattie's return came on a day all
  should remember,
A nasty day in the middle of September:
Thunderstorms, hail, and tornadic winds
Unleashed lightning bolts that disturbed her
  Zen,
Sending flooding high tides into her cypress
  den,
Awakening the little anger that still resided
  within.
Emerging from the tree that was her coffin,
Her animosity stirred with memories almost
  forgotten:

A similar day, she started to recall.
Then she remembered more. Then she
  remembered all
About the day when more than Hell's fury she
  brought to those ghosts:
Typhoons and terror, she massacred most
During the battle of the spirits at St. Augustine's
  old fort,
When she laughed at the Devil and to God did
  retort:

"I've won the final battle; I've won the war!
Satan's no match for me, not any more.

I demand my own kingdom, similar to Hell;
I demand a legend, a story to tell;
I demand all this, or I'll do even more
To annihilate your earth with blood and gore
And crush those pathetic minions you so adore!"

As all now know, God bit His tongue,
Knowing full well that Hattie had won.
He gave her the swamps on the St. Johns River,
A glowing dark eye, a smell worse than liver,
A reputation for evil-- a legend of her own.
She now had a kingdom for the evil she'd
    sown:
Far better a place where she'd be all alone
Than sent back to Hades with more devils to
    clone.

Chapter 3

The Sorcerers' Clan

The howling gales and pelting hail
Dashed her reminiscence, and she began to
rail
At her ugliness and loneliness and inescapable
plight,
When her flickering tongue tasted something
not quite right.
Awakening more she arose from her stupor:

"A goat? A gator? Maybe a grouper?
What do I taste? What do I smell?
It's so very tough to tell…
A snake, a toad, a turtle, a lizard?
No, by damn, it's a warlock wizard!"

Summoning all her remaining powers,
She followed the scent trail for what seemed
like hours.
Suddenly, hearing a long forgotten sound,
She submerged in the muck and put her ear to
hard ground:
"A voodoo priest, singing chants and
incantations!
Another silly fool who faces ablation!"

Now stirred to action
And wanting satisfaction

Her adrenaline flowed, and her bile gushed
    forth.
Her spirit ascended and leered to the north;
Its beacon eye spied a spigot of spiraling
    smoke.
Returning to Swamp Hattie, her spirit bowed
    and spoke:

"A black magic prince
Burning peat and incense:
The odor's sickening-sweet and so intense.
It beckons to you, as a pretense."

Energized and having a need to fill--
It had been so long since a successful kill--
She skated the waters to a black oak hammock
    island
Where she paused to size up this strange little
    band,
And she detected the presence of a medicine
    man:

"A Seminole shaman doing all that he can
To tap my psyche, to read my mind.
Four different sorcerers, how intertwined?"

Assuming her most ghastly, grotesque form,

She evaporated from site, which was her norm,
Then materialized instantly in front of this
    group.
Each fell to his knees with heads in a stoop.
The Seminole witch doctor, barely raising his
    eyes,
With quivering voice cried out in surprise:

"Swamp Hattie! At last! You do survive!
You're colder than Death but clearly alive!
You make the Grim Reaper seem like Mickey
    Mouse!
A statue you need in Potter's house!
You're even more grotesque than I've ever been
    told!
Your hideous beauty is a thing to behold!"

Hattie's tongue flickered and tasted the air,
"These beings have power; I must be aware."

Scanning their thoughts she could not make
    connection,
So she surrounded them all from every
    direction;
She fixed on their eyes,
So they knew she despised
    ...their presence in her Kingdom!

"Enough of your crap! Why are you here?
Speak the truth, as you have much to fear!
I'll listen to you, to all your bunch,
But make it quick, or I'll have you for brunch!"

Levitating each one from the land
And binding them tight with gator leather
  bands,
She pried open their brains with a wave of her
  hand,
And one by one they told her their tales:
How they found each other and followed her
  trail
In hopes of finding her –– their Holy Grail!

Chapter 4

The Black Magic Prince

The Seminole witch doctor then spoke again,
Introducing the group: first, the black magic
     man.
Robed all in black with nary a hair,
Dark sunglasses worn with a flair,
Mahogany skin tones, a handsome young man,
Obeying Hattie's orders, he quickly began.

"My mother died young, a gruesome murder
     quite tragic;
So I turned to the Dark Side and learned black
     magic.
The Caribbean's my world; the islands, my
     realm.
I controlled all trade; I was at the helm.
I sailed and surfed from atoll to atoll,
Extracting bribes, tariffs, and terrible tolls,
Growing rich and powerful and then I
     discovered
Black magic potions that easily cover
Anything and everything, even smells such as
     yours.
Yes, Swamp Hattie, I can block your pores.
No longer will they ooze that horrible stench
That so often throws an unwelcomed wrench
Into the terror that your hatred brings,
Into your ways of killing things.

Now you can sneak-up on a steer;
Now you can surprise even a deer;
Now you can snatch little kids with no fear
That your smell will ever give you away.
This is the beginning of a new day.
God cast me out because of my greed;
I want to go back; I want to be freed!"

Dennis M. Smith Jr.

Chapter 5

The
Wee Warlock
Wizard

"Now you, you wee warlock wizard.
Deliver your thoughts, or you'll eat your own
gizzard!"

Trembling and shaking and stuttering with
fright,
In spite of the bands that bound him so tight,
He tinkled in his pants! They turned yellow-
green,
Which contrasted nicely with the purplest robe
ever seen.
The wizard was frail, short, absolutely lean.
His sparkling white hat no longer matched his
jeans.
He sweated so profusely he glowed with a
sheen--
Hard to imagine he could possibly be mean.
So wimpy, in fact, he'd be a poor excuse for a
gnome
Or even a leprechaun of the Irish's golden
dome.
Clearly, this wizard kind of wished he were
home.

"I've dreamed of the day that I'd see that eye;
I feared so much that first I would die

Before meeting you -- the legend that shaped
  my life."

"Enough of your sniveling, whimpering ways!
Get on with whatever you have to say!"

"My mother was a witch; my father, a wizard.
They created secret potions from roaches, bats,
   and lizards.
The spells of Narnia were all their doing:
A result of their recipes and special brewing.
The Witches of Winter, they created them, too,
All through the use of their secret brews.
They taught me their craft, and I learned it
   well.
Remember how the Empire fell?
The black plague of Europe? My stories to tell.
I hated all men; they made fun of me.
So even I got, as you can see."

"God finally tired of my kind of fun.
'Warlock,' he said, 'Your day is done.'
Sentenced me to life, to permanent exile;
Destroyed my records; set fire to my files.
But two formulae stayed in my head:
One masks all light; one resurrects the dead.
For you Swamp Hattie, I can hide your eye;
You will still see fine, though I know not why.
With your eye well hidden and your stench
   dispersed,
The warning signs to others will be reversed!"

Chapter 6

The Voodoo Priest

The voodoo priest, draped with white shrouds,
Hovered in her shackles quite close to the
  clouds.
Her lustrous black beauty hid the evil within:
An evil much darker than the tone of her skin.
Her Marley dreadlocks hung down to her toes;
Her pincushion dolls told tales of much woe.
It was her time; she was next in line.
So she started to speak and then to opine:

"Louisiana's swamps are my domain.
I lead the few spirits there that remain
In the graveyards of the Crescent City.
Our numbers are falling; it's such a pity.
And our powers fade
As God has forbade
That we do no more evil than we do good.
So I left my swamps and I left my woods.
I had heard of your legend and your plight,
And, while my magic has faded, I still have the
  might
To make you a chameleon, to hide you from
  sight:
Hide you so well
That no one could tell
Who you are, what you are, or even where!
Not humans, not Satan, not even God up

there!
God cast me out; I want to return from the
   fringe.
God cast me out! I want revenge!"

Chapter 7

The
Seminole Medicine
Man

The Seminole shaman gowned in garnet and
   gold
Brandished a spear that was centuries old.
It provided his tribes with meat and 'taters,
Protection included, except for the 'Gators.
His weathered tanned hides told of great age:
A powerful being, a soothsayer, and sage.
Hattie understood that he was one of the very
   few
Whose powers could lead and control such a
   crew.
She studied and analyzed all of his moves
By searching his cerebrum to its uncinate
   groove.
She scanned his brain thoroughly so no secrets
   remained;
Then she commanded him to recite his
   personal refrain.

"I, Swamp Hattie, have lived in despair;
I have known for centuries your private lair
But could not find you anywhere.
None of my magic could find a way
To locate you or where you stay.
I feared you were gone as the humans say.

I used all my powers to summon my
  friends,
To bring them together, and to have them
  attend

A seance with sorcerers long since deceased
Designed to learn how to significantly increase
Our chances of successfully contacting you."

"Combining our convocation's collective
   powers,
We plotted and planned for hours and hours
And decided to duplicate
And somehow recreate
That terrible storm of your finest hour
When the Devil and his sidekicks ran and
   cowered.
The night you proved you were the one;
The night your legend was finally won.
We surmised that the weather would
   unencumber
The stupor brought on by your deep slumber,
And the storm would unleash that beautiful
   beast
That none has seen since your terror ceased.
We guessed right, because here you are.
My contribution, which is somewhat bizarre,
Is not brews, magic, or potions;
It's not spells, chants, or lotions;
My role as a Seminole medicine man
Is that I have a proposal…a calculated plan."

Chapter 8

The Medicine Man's Plan

Keeping them aloft, physically and mentally
   bound,
Hattie interrogated the group without uttering
   a sound:

"I'm somewhat impressed, but equally
   depressed,
That your ruse worked, which I cannot contest.
But it leaves me wondering and wildly
   distressed
That my powers are waning; they have seen
   their best.
You came here under great risk to your health;
You came in the open without hiding or
   stealth.
But your stories are interesting, so I must hear
   your plan.
Speak to me now, Seminole medicine man."

Using mental mind-locks the shaman began
With the subtle details of his master plan:

"Listen real closely; listen to me!
This is our chance to at last be free.
Everyone thinks Swamp Hattie is dead;
They've celebrated that thought to which they
   are wed.

We'll use this fact as the very core
Of our strategy to wage silent war.
To start, the Prince will block your smell;
Then the wizard will hide your eye as well.
And a chameleon curse from the voodoo
     priest
Will shield you from all, to say the least.
No one will know that you really exist
Or that your powers still persist.
With this cover
No one will discover
That the death and destruction we secretly deal
Comes from you, Swamp Hattie, and the
     power you wield.
Unlike the past where you tortured your prey,
Where you scared your victims by night and
     day,
Where you bragged and boasted and used fear
     to slay,
Now you'll work undercover and never give
     away
The truth that Swamp Hattie is alive and
     strong
And that nothing in life is safe from the wrong
That you can wreak every night and all the day
     long.
Most will think it's just Nature, fate, or bad

luck,
Or that life's not fair; that life just sucks.
And all the while we'll continue our spree
Of plundering, pillaging, killing, too...
      ...invisible terrorists, we!"

"An interesting proposal, but what's in it for
      you?
What do you want, you and your crew?"

"Just what we said: it's revenge we seek;
That and to watch the havoc you'll wreak.
Using the same magic that will free up your
      power,
We'll use it ourselves and be home in an hour.
We'll shake the rust from our corroded bones;
We'll expand our reach and retake our thrones!
And you, Swamp Hattie, our Queen you'll be,
Ruling the earth, land, air and sea --
A role we believe you deserve so well.
Under your watch, Earth will be Hell!"

"I like your thinking and I love your plan.
Welcome to *my* kingdom; welcome to *my*
      clan!"

With those words Hattie released her lock,

Freeing their brains, bonds, and blocks.
As the winds howled and the storm roared,
Hattie and the sorcerers suddenly soared,
Whirling and writhing and spinning about
They chanted and moaned and began to tout
The genius of their collective ways:
The coming of more terror and "happier" days!

Chapter 9

Swamp Hattie's Lair

Energized and revitalized by her motley crew
And anticipating all the evil she'd do,
Hattie parted the storm with a wave of her
   hand
And returned to her swamp, she and her band.

The weather raged on, except in Hattie's lair,
Where darkness was pure ebony beyond
   compare.
The silence was deafening , as intense as
   could be;
The temperature, cold, like death times three.
Inside her old cypress protected from spies,
Hattie wrapped them in her mind-lock,
   then looked into their eyes:

"Gather round my ice fire and enjoy its smoke;
Inhale deeply and try not to choke.
But perform your magic; do it now!
You have one chance only; that's all I'll allow!"

Dennis M. Smith Jr.

Chapter 10

The Black Magic Potion

The black magic prince opened his mind;
Out poured his thoughts, which were one of a
  kind.

"To you, Swamp Hattie, I freely bequeath
The family recipe that'll bring anguish and
  grief
To the humans of this world and the spirits
  beneath.
Begin by extracting 13 living teeth
From the jaws of a child, not from on top but
  underneath.
Grind them with your gruesome gums,
Then grind them some more, and spit out the
  crumbs.
Collect them in a bottle of Bacardi's best rum.
Harvest the snot from a pure Cracker cow;
Add it to the bile from a feral hog sow.
Snip yellow jasmine, not the flowers, but the
  vine.
Mix all ingredients; then shake to combine.
Pour this magic potion onto your mossy head;
Let it drip down until your face turns brilliant
  red.
Use your forked tongue to lick and then spread
The lotion all over your body, and, if you've
  done as I've said,

Your odor will vanish; you'll not smell of the
dead!"

Leaving her troops bound in her mind-lock,
She teleported herself faster than time on a
clock,
Collected all materials, and returned to the
group,
Where she concocted the formula, just like
chicken soup.

Following the princely directions as closely as
could be,
She counted to one, then two, and finally three,
And, pouring the liquor onto her hair,
Her face turned as crimson as a Bryant bear.
Then, using her tongue and spreading it
everywhere,
She drew a deep breath and became acutely
aware
That her smell was gone…vanished… into thin
air!

"You've earned your reward, Prince; you soon
may go!
With my powers, on you I bestow
Free reign of your kingdom, and, please know,

If you ever need me, come disguised as a crow."

"Thank you, Queen Hattie, I shall do as you
  say;
Soon I'll be off to my islands without delay,
But I wish to see the others' tricks. Do you
  mind if I stay?"
Confirming his intentions with a look in his
  brain,
Hattie motioned to all that the Prince could
  remain.

Chapter 11

The Wizard's Brew

The wimpy wizard's thoughts came pouring
  out next:

"With my family's brew I'll end your cruel hex;
I'll douse that eye's glow with which you've
  been vexed.
I only have two formulae that I still remember,
The one you want works well in September;
The other one only functions in the time of
  December.
Fortunately, Hattie, you have no use for
  reclaiming the dead,
So rather than messing with two, we'll work on
  one instead."

"Come on, my wimpy warlock wizard! I don't
  like you!
Get on with your work. Do your do! Make up
  that brew!"

Mortified by the fierceness of Hattie's thoughts
  -- it was clear she didn't like him, even with
  the help he brought --
His mind waves stuttered, then stammered so
  slowly out
That Hattie entered his brain and turned it
  about!

By making such a maneuver she left no doubt
Of what she thought of this lousy little lout.
Her tactic worked, and his words found a route
To escape the muddled neurons
Of this mighty midget moron!

The wizard began chanting in unintelligible
   tongues,
Then screaming quite loudly at the top of his
   lungs:

"Bring me a kettle
Of gleaming gold metal.
Fill it with the dung
Of 13 newborn young
Of midnight black felines.
Then make a beeline
To accumulate the blood
And associated crud
From the pulverized corpses
Of two freshly slain horses.
Pour this slurry into the pot,
And boil and simmer until it's blistering hot.
While it bubbles, find me 13 nine-year-old
   boys:
Extract their eyeballs and bring me their toys.
I need beauty marks from 13 teenage girls;

Rip them out whole, the size of large pearls.
I'll add these ingredients, one at a time;
Then, I'll insert my cane and recite my rhyme.
So begone Swamp Hattie; bring me this stuff,
Exactly what I asked for; exactly enough."

With her malodorous gases a thing of the past,
Hattie took to her tasks and finished them fast.
Laying the ingredients at the foot of the
    wizard,
She reached down his throat and grasped his
    gizzard:

"This better work, you little twerp!
Or my bile you will taste, slurp upon slurp!"

"Let me begin, and soon, my Queen,
You'll have an eye that sees but cannot be
    seen."

With these thoughts he filled the metal kettle,
Stirring all the while so the contents would not
    settle.
Completing his list, he inserted his cane,
Entered a trance, and grimaced with pain:

"Obiwan, ichiwan,

Beacon be gone!
Omatell, idagell,
Hide it so well.
Itchibee, ophthapee,
So no one can see.
Googere, ocstafre,
But it still works for thee!"

"Now, Swamp Hattie, put your scepter in there,
And add to the pot, one long eyelash hair."

Following his instructions to the letter of the
   law,
The sorcerer band could not believe what they
   saw:
A thunderous bolt of prickly heat lightning
Struck the wizard's cane -- it was quite
   frightening,
Electrifying the warlock and his bubbling
   brew,
Sending steam and ashes and this boiling goo
All over Swamp Hattie, now one screaming
   shrew!

"You stupid dumb wizard, what the Hell did
   you do?!!!"

"All part of my plan, I assure you my Queen.
Now, one last thing to complete my scheme."

Gathering the steam in the palm of his hand
And adding a tear from one Meibomian gland,
A golden orange pepper the size of a thumb
Materialized from nowhere, from where did it
    come?
Cutting off its cap, he filled it with goo,
Handed it to Hattie and said, "Chew it now!
    Chew!"
The heat from the datil put sweat on her brow,
The beads became torrents, no one knows
    quite how.
Foul and acidic, they swirled in her eye,
Dousing its beacon on the very first try!
Loving the taste of this datil pepper sauce,
Hattie licked all traces from her hair of
    Spanish moss.
Handing Hattie a mirror to look at herself,
The warlock wizard, like some silly elf,
Danced and chortled about his success
And about the powers with which he'd been
    blessed.

Hattie glanced in the glass, which instantly
  cracked,
But it revealed to Hattie what her eye lacked:
No light from her eye -- not a hint of a glow.
She could see fine -- how did it know?
So the wee warlock wizard after all was right:
Now, no smelly warnings by day; no beacon
  lights by night!

Chapter 12

The Voodoo Hex

The Medicine man telepathisized,

"We've taken care of your eyes;
We've eliminated your smell;
All is fine; it goes well.
Now, it's the voodoo priest's time
To assist with our crime.
A chameleon you'll become
That will cloak and hide you from
All eyes, everywhere,
Both down below and up there,
So neither Heaven nor Hell
Will ever be able to tell
Where you are or what you're doing,
Trouble you cause or evil you're brewing.
Two for two certainly isn't bad,
But what comes next is the biggest challenge
    we've had."

Hattie remained silent, her brain a complete
    blank.
She enjoyed a deep breath that no longer
    stank.
She gave no clue to the rest of the crew
That she had real doubts about what the
    voodoo priest could do.

Sensing the emptiness and knowing it meant
   trouble,
The voodoo magic came fast, came on the
   double:

"I know you have doubts what I can do with
   my dolls.
But this is my time; it happens each Fall,
For as long as I can remember, as long as I can
   recall.
So release my bonds; release my mind,
And I'll make you, my Hattie, impossible to
   find!"

Feeling quite kindred to another swamp being
And having seen no signs of anyone fleeing,
Hattie did as she was asked,
Freeing the priest to prepare for her task.

Reaching into the boggy, swampy muck,
A handful of clay she carefully plucked
From the mud below those dank, dark pools.
Shaping it sharply with her own drool
And using her fingers as her only tools,
She fashioned a miniature of Swamp Hattie,
Complete with moss hair and a tiny cow patty.
She spoke not a word, but the swamp still

knew
That something quite powerful was abrew
For the storm that had parted for this motley
    crew
Became fiercer and fiercer after starting anew.
The swamp exploded as its creatures screeched
    out
And a vortex of violence formed a spout,
Sucked them all in, and tossed them about.
Then it hurled them and whirled them around
    and around,
Creating terror and fear and the most ungodly
    sounds
As they went up and up and around and
    around!

Taking Hattie's hand and holding it tight,
Squeezing it hard with all of her might,
The priest, the doll, and Swamp Hattie,
Who held between her teeth that tiny cow
    patty,
Pierced the wall of the vortex and entered the
    tornado,
Which had the most treacherous winds ever
    east of Laredo.
Inside the funnel in the eye of the storm,
Hattie found that the temperature was

surprisingly warm,
And she noticed that the doll began to change form.
First one shape; then another;
Many different hues; many different colors;
Changing so quickly, how could it possibly be?
So Hattie watched intently only to see
The priest pluck a pine needle from off her chin
And impale the clay being with this natural pin.
Flinging her creation into the tornado's spinning wall,
It disappeared up the tube, which ended the squall;
In fact, all the storms ended, for once and for all.
With the calm came a deafening quiet,
And what followed next was simply a riot.

When the storms departed, Hattie's mind-locks went, too.
The shaman, the wizard, and the prince each knew
That something profound had just taken place.
There was no sign of Swamp Hattie: no smell, no eye, no face.

She had disappeared with nary a trace!
Only the voodoo priest remained, and the
   others implored her to replace
Their questions and worries and, in any case,
To explain what had happened and just taken
   place.

The Seminole medicine man, quickly losing
   his cool,
Asked, "What have you done you lunatic fool?
She's gone! She's gone! You've ended her rule!"

Replying not, the priest took a knee,
And grasping beads of gold, purple, and green,
She put forth her hand where it could be seen.
After a moment…the beads began to rise,
Straight up from her palm to the level of her
   eyes;
Suspended in mid-air, the beads swung to and
   fro,
Then disappeared quietly, where did they go?

The medicine man spoke, not happy at all,
"Enough of your magic; you really have the
   gall.
Give us some answers; why do you stall?"

Suddenly the shaman, wizard, and prince
Found themselves pinned to a pink picket
  fence,
Unable to move or use any sense
To determine the facts or other pretense
As to why or why not this voodoo priest
Could have developed such power that, at the
  very least,
Prevented them from escaping and being
  released.
Mere seconds passed before the answer came:
A blood-curdling cackle crashed their brains,
And Swamp Hattie materialized out of
  nowhere.
The three sorcerers could not help but stare
At the strand of gold, purple, and green,
Like the beads of the Cajuns of New Orleans,
That entwined her wrist like some serpentine
  machine.
As they fixated on Hattie's long bony wrist,
Each began to chuckle as they got the gist
Of the trick the priest had perfectly planned
To demonstrate to Hattie's clandestine clan
This awesome new weapon that Hattie now
  had
To cloak her detection -- they were so glad!
What an incredible asset with which to do bad!

The voodoo priest rose from her kneeling
   stance;
Peering at Hattie with a side-ways glance,
She explained to all that the voodoo beads
Were secret, sacred chameleon seeds
That rendered her invisible to one and to all,
Including God and the Devil, who could no
   longer forestall,
Recognizing what loomed ahead that could
   lead to their fall!

Chapter 13

Swamp Hattie's
Proclamation

Swamp Hattie then freed them from the fence
And proclaimed to her tribe that from this day hence
The Earth would change:
She would rearrange
All the world's order, and she would ordain
That life, as we know it, would not remain.

"My powers are complete; I shall begin my reign
Of torture, terror, terrible times, and great pain.
No one will know that it's I at the helm
Until it's too late, and then I'll overwhelm
All living beings, spirits, Satan, and the three I want most:
The Father, the Son, and the Holy Ghost!"

You have done your part;
You are free to depart.
You have earned your freedoms;
Return to your kingdoms.
The dies are all cast:
Earth's future is past!"

With these words the sorcerers dispersed
Knowing full well to come was the worst

That this globe would suffer, curse upon curse;
That no salve would heal or medicine nurse;
That the globe would soon understand
What north Florida suffered under Hattie's
  hand;
That Hattie's hate would flood all over the land
And her death and destruction would expand
  and expand...

        ...until the earth ripped apart!

Epilogue

So beware Hattie's words when you view TV
news:
Know that the stories are really direct clues
That confirm and support
Swamp Hattie's ultimate retort:

"The dies are all cast.
Earth's future is past!"

The End

Book 2

The Wrath and Redemption of *Swamp Hattie*

Book 3 of the Swamp Hattie Trilogy

Chapter 1

Swamp Hattie
Reminisces

Swamp Hattie posed above a bluff overlooking
  the Old Man River,
Contemplating the pain she was about to
  deliver.
She snarled at the sky as the sun sank down,
As billowing thunderheads silhouetted the
  River Town.
Ole King Cotton had nary a clue
About what Swamp Hattie was about to do.

Then Hattie paused to reminisce and
   remember…

That nasty day in September
Which made her not just a pretender
But truly the leading contender
For being the most wicked, evil force
From history's beginning and throughout its
   course.
Her memory flashed back to many centuries
   ago,
When her sailor lover jilted her so
By leaving St. Augustine without a "goodbye,"
Without an excuse, or reason why.
Crushed and broken-hearted, Hattie decided to
   die:
She took her own life because of that sailor guy.
Because of the hate she possessed while she
   lived,
Heaven and St. Peter refused to give
Her admittance through the pearly gates
And sent her to Hades where she honed her hate
To such a sharpness that the Devil himself
Labeled her a monster, a witch, a murderous elf,
A ghoul, a goblin, a supreme evil being,
So despicable, in fact, that Satan started seeing
That there was no room even in Hell

*For something like Swamp Hattie that loved evil
    so well.*
So back to St. Augustine, Satan exiled this soul,
To haunt and taunt and to take a toll
On the inhabitants of the City of Old.
But Hattie's antics even scared the other ghosts;
*They challenged her to battle at the Fort on the
    coast.*
*She massacred these spirits and made God
    decree*
*That a kingdom for Swamp Hattie be given to
    her free.*
God and the Devil decided to give her
*The swamps between the ocean and the St.
    Johns River.*
*To protect all living things from this wicked
    wench,*
They gave Swamp Hattie a terrible stench.
They also gave her a beacon eye,
Something for people to easily spy.
They did these things and made her ugly, too,
To help limit the evil and damage she'd do.
Hattie ruled her domain with terror and strife.
She depleted her swamp of all of its life,
Killing with hate… no need for a knife…
Hate for the sailor who ruined her life.
As life disappeared, so did her fun.

She grew bored, depressed, and eternally glum.
She took very long naps, a hibernation of sorts;
Hattie vanished from sight; there were no
* reports.*
Everyone forgot that she even existed.
Rumors of her legend just barely persisted.
Then came that day of her resurrection
When a sorcerers' band ended her dejection--
A band that included a black magic prince and
* a voodoo priest,*
A warlock wizard and a Seminole witch doctor,
* who always came last but was never least--*
All afraid of Swamp Hattie, afraid of this
* wretched soul, afraid of this fearsome beast.*
They cast miraculous, magical, mystical spells
That worked so incredibly, wonderfully well
That Swamp Hattie became a chameleon so no
* one could tell*
Who she was, what she was, or where she could
* be:*
They could not smell her anymore nor could
* they see.*
So Hattie slipped away from her swampy
* domain,*
Became a silent killer, and began the terrorists'
* game*
Of randomized destruction aimed to destroy

and maim
As much and as many as she could possibly
claim.
Not even God and the Devil knew now what
Hattie could do.
Her powers were potent, thanks to her sorcerers'
crew.
She targeted Florida, then spread 'round the
earth
Doing evil and destruction for all she was
worth!

From the wild, wild weather of the tropical
storms
To the crime rates way beyond norms;
From the disemboweled bodies and the
decapitated horses
To massive wild fires with unknown sources;
To abandoned young children found buried on
golf courses;
From devastating Andrew and F-4 tornadoes
To deadly draughts and contaminated
tomatoes;
From '89's snows and killing frosts
To countless lives on I-95 lost;
From the bleeding cross on Hospital Creek
To devilish red tides that killed both strong

and weak;
From Bayard's silhouettes to Skynard's fatal
crash
To a polluted St. Johns loaded with trash
To exploding space shuttles and meteor near
misses:
All spawned from the womb of Hattie's abysses.

Just a partial list, to name but a few.
The signs were there, more subtle it's true.
She learned new lessons; give her her due.
Swamp Hattie no longer sought public acclaim
For what she did or whom she maimed.
She cared not that no one knew of her great
success.
It made it just that much easier to cause
distress,
Death, destruction, and enduring duress.
The above small sampling tells the true tale
Of why Swamp Hattie's legend finally paled:
She had assumed a silent, secretive style,
That succeeded always, not just once in a
while.
Yet the clues were all there, clue after clue:
Messages to me and signs to you.
By abandoning old ways, she was reborn.
By learning new ways, she was transformed.

Chapter 2

The New Madrid Fault

Swamp Hattie trashed her reminiscing;
Then, with much grunting and hissing,
She inserted her staff into the river's mud
And sucked out three pints of raw crawfish
   blood.
After swilling down this gruesome crud,
She thrust her arm toward a storm that was
   brewing,
A storm that was rotating, swirling, and
   stewing,
A storm that was intent on accruing and
   renewing
Hattie's love of massive, living-grave
   viewings--
A special storm of Swamp Hattie's doing!

Extending the index finger of her boney left
   hand,
Her long sharp nail began to expand
And extend toward the cumulonimbus clouds
That grumbled loudly, then louder than loud.
And when the nail was longer than the eye
   could see,
The storm let loose with what could only be
The most gargantuan discharge of static volts
To ever deliver shocks and electrical jolts,
Enough to confuse and scramble every single

mind
In the history of this planet and of mankind.
Hattie simply giggled;
Her body barely wiggled;
Then, she laughed and chortled right out loud,
As she absorbed the energy from the clouds.
Retracting her nail
Like the head of a snail,
She lowered her arm as it began to hail.
Grasping a hailstone in her gnarled fist,
She squeezed it firmly and gave it a twist.
It melted slowly into the ground
Making a deep, deep hole until it found
The firm bedrock of the New Madrid Fault,
The foundational structure that Swamp Hattie
   sought.
Inserting her arm down into the hole,
Hattie elongated her finger to find its goal:
The hard layers of the tectonic plate
That Hattie needed to seal the fate
Of the Mid-South's premier city.
It was her target; there would be no pity.

Hattie drilled her nail down through the shale
And into stony hardness that makes diamonds
   pale.
She discharged the energy from the

thunderbolt
That delivered such a violent jolt
Of trillions and trillions and trillions of joules
-- the perfect effecter, the perfect tool --
That a cataclysmic sequence of events
Resulted in a series of tears, rips, and rents
That ended with the lithosphere swallowing whole
A city of millions, FedEx, King Cotton, the Liberty Bowl,
Handy's Beale Street, barbecue, Elvis, music with soul:
All disappeared completely down a black hole!
The rushing reddish river carried all to their death;
It sucked them all down and sucked out their breath.
Everything was gone; absolutely nothing was left.
Hattie cackled with satisfaction
At the exactness of her extraction
Of an entire town of the mid-nation;
She simply could not express her elation
That a new canyon grander than grand
Now marked the spot where the city used to stand.
All went perfectly according to plan,

according to text --
A city was child's play!
California would be next!

Chapter 3

The Sorcerers Rebel!

As Swamp Hattie enjoyed the view of the
  fruits of her labor,
Her flickering tongue tasted an unusual flavor,
One that evoked memories of spirits she
  savored
And magical memories of friends she favored.
Sensing their presence even before they
  appeared,
Swamp Hattie knew her sorcerer gang was
  near.
The priest and prince materialized together,
Followed by the witch doctor dragging a
  tether
Attached to which was one wee warlock
  wizard,
Who still feared Hattie had plans for his
  gizzard.

"Welcome, my friends!
Just where have you been?
I hope you take measure
And a great dose of pleasure
Of what you've made possible for me to do.
As a result of your potions, your magic, and
  your brews,
I've executed our demolition terrorism plan,
The one devised by you, Seminole medicine

man.
Now, it's time to crush and completely destroy
This sacred living sphere…God's favorite little
    toy!"

The Seminole shaman showed deep respect,
Bowed to Swamp Hattie, but then began to
    detect
That Swamp Hattie had sensed just why they
    had come.
No time to delay, no time to play dumb!

"Swamp Hattie, our Queen,
It can clearly be seen
That you rule what's left of this planet Earth
From pole to pole and around its girth.
Nothing can stop you. This is your home turf.
You own the lakes, rivers, seas, and surf.
You cause death and ill.
You kill for the thrill.
You conquer at will.
Neither God in Heaven nor the Devil down
    below
Knows it's you at the helm of this demolition
    show.
For all these reasons, you're a huge success.
For all these reasons, we come with a request.

Your tantrums and tirades now threaten us,
   they do.
Our kingdoms are dwindling; our minions,
   too.
Your acts have become increasingly cruel,
Leaving little doubt they will certainly fuel
A firestorm that will bring one final duel
       …with Him.

So we fear for ourselves and all those we rule.
Now, God has come searching for answers and
   clues
As to why all this is happening -- He's in a true
   stew.
We've taken refuge in a remote location
Trying to avoid any possible confrontation
       …with Him.
We now ask you Swamp Hattie, as our leader
   and queen:
Please stop your assault before we are seen.
It's time to *stop*; there can be no in-between!"

Dennis M. Smith Jr.

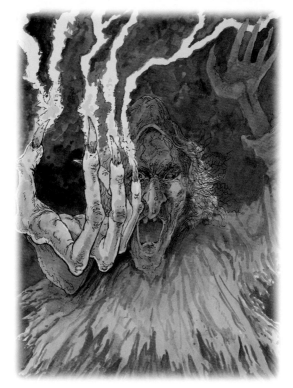

Hattie erupted in anger; lightning bolts
  sparked from her nails.
Her eyes shot darts, as her arms wheeled and
  flailed
So violently they created wind gusts and gales
Complete with thunder and grapefruit-sized
  hail

That fell all around as Swamp Hattie screamed
   and railed!

"Traitors, you are! I can't believe what I heard!
Not a sentence, not a phrase, not one single
   word!
You wish to save His helpless herd?
Well! Be gone with your group, you Seminole
   nerd!
You're nothing but a bunch of worthless
   warlock turds!
Get out of my sight! And beyond my reach!
Be gone, before I piss on you each
And give you a lesson you'll be unable to
   teach!"

With her warning Hattie commenced whirling
   around.
Faster, then faster, then faster than sound,
Generating white heat that melted the ground.
Her actions translated clearly to "Nope!"
Which answered their request, ended their
   hope,
And left only the reality with which they must
   cope:
Swamp Hattie had departed without a trace,
Intending to end the entire human race!

Chapter 4

Swamp Hattie
Warns Satan

Swamp Hattie surveyed from atop Mount
   Everest
The results of her many terrorist quests.
Her lips snarled as she cackled aloud:

"What I see makes me so proud!
Rips torn all through the Earth's thin, measly
   crust;
Fires and brimstones that bubble and burst
And bleed onto what little land is left,
As the oceans keep rising like treble clefs.
While global warming was a convenient
   excuse,
My hot breath was the true cause of the abuse
That caused the melting of the polar ice caps
That resulted in conservatives taking the rap.
And with my floods
The globe's life blood--
Freshwater needed to sustain all life--
Became scarcer and scarcer which created
   great strife,
Resulting in battles and terrible wars
That slaughtered millions and millions and
   literally tore
The brotherhood of Man apart at its core.
It is now time to change the pecking order!
Let's see how Satan likes being confined by a

border!"

Swamp Hattie hacked up a slug of phlegmatic
    gruel
And spat it out with a glob of dark sticky
    drool.
The stuff bubbled and hissed and smelled like
    diesel fuel,
So volatile and acidic, it became a driller's tool
That oozed through the ground, going deep,
    deep down,
Where it eventually found, like an amorphous
    blood hound…
                    …the Devil himself!

Following the rent her juices bored in the
    earth,
Swamp Hattie snuck up on Satan and with
    great mirth
Materialized from nowhere right in front of
    his eyes --
Nose to nose, navel to navel, and thighs to
    thighs!

She scared the red demon so badly, he turned
   white as a ghost
And fainted so completely, he was as limp as
   milk toast!

Swamp Hattie kissed him on the lips and
　　breathed on his face,
An act which closely mimics being sprayed
　　with mace
And an act which aroused the groggy, great,
　　horned-one,
Who turned redder than ever…a victim of
　　Hattie's fun!

"Bellowing Beelzebub! What in my Hell brings
　　you here?
Or am I having nightmares from too much of
　　Beelze's beer?
On second thought, I don't want to hear,
But I'm sure you'll tell me anyway, my
　　Hattie dear.
Let me make it absolutely, positively, perfectly
　　clear
That it was God's ideas to make your looks so
　　queer,
To exile you to the swamps for so many, many
　　years,
To isolate you from all of your ghostly peers,
And to make everyone and everything
　　eternally fear… you!
I thought you were history!
Yesterday's stale mystery!"

"You and everyone else! But that's where you
   were wrong!

While you and God slept, I grew stronger than
   strong!

Now, I go everywhere, even where I don't
   belong.

And you, Satan, and all of your Hell-bound
   throng

Can no longer compete with me -- I am that
   strong!

From the Third Reich's rise and its Holocaust
   Hell

To the crack in Philly's Liberty Bell;

From the Twin Tower attacks

To the war in Iraq;

From the financial Armageddon

To the French Revolution's beheadings;

From the nuclear secrets that led to the Bomb

That destroyed Man's sleep, his peace, and his
   calm;

From swine flu epidemics and HIV mutations

To massive tsunamis that swamped whole
   nations;

From assassinations of world leaders

To deadly viral infections of free bleeders:

These were not mere accidents or acts of

Nature or Mankind;
These were products of my genius; they were
    all acts of mine!
I come to warn you today: stay out of my way!
For when I return to the surface, it will be
    God's turn to pay.
I will challenge Him to fight.
Then, I'll blast him from sight!
His universe will be mine
From now on and for all time.
I give you one chance to save your own Hell
Because you taught me my skills and you
    taught me so well.
Do not misunderstand! Because, if you fail,
You will meet your end... I shall prevail!"

"With you, Swamp Hattie, I want no
    confrontation.
I will stay down here and tend my
    Netherworld nation,
As you and God annihilate His favorite
    creation,
The very thought of which brings me great
    elation!
I have nothing more to say.
So please! Please! Just go away!"

Hattie spoke again before exiting Hades' door:
"Save this bracelet; you know who it is for.
I have cloned its secrets; I can make more.
Besides, you'll need all the help you can get,
Especially, if my warning you forget!"

Enveloping herself in a great ball of flames,
Swamp Hattie vanished more quickly than she came.
Observing trails of black soot and acrid ebony smoke,
Satan deeply inhaled and took a toke
Only to gasp and to literally choke
At the taste of the gases that would make mortal man croak.
As the Devil coughed, hacked, and violently gagged,
A single frigid breath from our evil spirit hag
Permeated all Hell
And penetrated so well
              …that Hell froze over!

Thawing the Devil with the mere energy of her thoughts,
Swamp Hattie reminded Satan of the warning she brought:
"Just a small sample of what I can do!

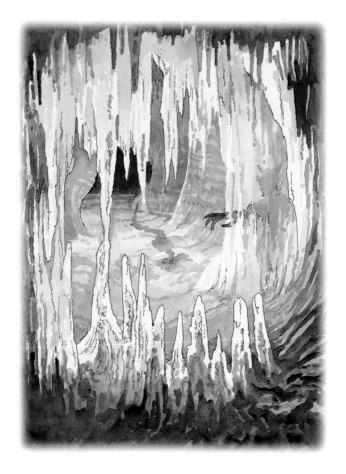

I trust you won't cross me, if you know what's
good for you!"

Chapter 5

Hattie Challenges God

Thrusting her arms toward the heavenly skies
With a smirking smile and glassy wild eyes,
Hattie challenged God to appear,
Expressed in His presence absolutely no fear,
And proclaimed Armageddon was undeniably
   here!

"You must be surprised that it was me!
For you could not sense or even see
That freely I roam your world and do great
   harm
To your children in cities, towns, and farms.
Let me tell you about what I've done,
Of the things I've done to have my fun!
It all started when a sorcerer clan
Came to me with magic and a secret plan
To douse my eye and cloak my smell,
Making me a chameleon so no one could tell
Where I was, who I was, or what I was doing,
Trouble I was causing, or spells I was brewing!
They executed their plan, and it worked so
   well
That here and now I proudly foretell
That your reign as the King of this world
Ends today because this 'ole girl
Has practiced more patience than that of Job
And is now in position to destroy your globe!

There is nothing you can do about it,
So listen as I proudly shout it!
Some of the things I've done without your
   knowing,
Some of the evil seeds I've been sowing,
I recite my list with more than a little crowing:

I know you remember
That day in December
When Pearl Harbor went up in smoke
As thousands died and croaked.
What about me playing terminator
At Daytona with Dale the Intimidator?
How about my ending Camelot?
Not too bad for just three shots!
And poor little Teddy went for a swim…
Must have been an angel watching over him!
Of course, Bobby wasn't so lucky,
As that plot went just ducky!
And how about all of Jonestown in a trance
As my poison took their last chance.
A jolly good time I had in the Atlantic
Where I sank the unsinkable ship Titanic
And watched as human ice cubes formed,
As those lucky few watched, cried, and
   mourned!
The forest fires of the Yellowstone caldera?

A more natural form of my home grown
terror.

The eruptions of Vesuvius and Mount St.
Helen?

Mere child's play for me and my band of
felons.

The mystery of the Bermuda Triangle?

No mystery at all when viewed from my angle!

I could go on and on and on for hours!
But I grow bored…it's time to show *You* my
  powers!
For now my powers exceed the Holy Ghost's,
And yours and your Sons as I possess the most
Black energy and evil than all time combined.
Evil so pure it cannot be refined,
Described, explained, or even defined!
I lay down my scepter in a show of defiance!
Time to show all there can be no reliance
On the Almighty God in Heaven above
Because, next to me, you're a meek turtle
  dove!
All will now know that their true judgment
  day
Comes not from their Maker but when I say!
And I say the time is here! Time to do away
With this failed earth
For which there clearly is a dearth
Of anything even remotely worth
                 …saving!

I challenge you to a duel:
You, your Sons, and that Holy Ghost fool!
A galactic battle for all to see!
Winner take all; that's how it will be!
When I'm finished, this globe will be gone:

No more sunsets, no more dawns!
Then I'll go on throughout your universe
Spreading fear and terror and even worse:
Destroying your Word, page by page, verse by
   verse!
Revenge will be mine for *Your* giving me this
   curse!"

Chapter 6

God Responds

"So it was you, Swamp Hattie, I should have
  known all along,
But my human dominions have done so much
  wrong,
So many, many times and for so very, very
  long,
That I thought they deserved these problems
  that they brought:
The famines, the floods, and the wars they
  fought;
The heat waves, the hurricanes, and the
  diseases they caught;
The horrors and the terrors from the gods they
  sought;
All the bad things their greed and hatred
  wrought.
That they were your doing, I had not that
  thought!

You're right, Hattie, there's not much left to
  save,
But, before I make ready earth's final grave,
There are still those few who are humble and
  brave,
Who lead good lives and know how to behave.
These are the ones I will fight to save.

I recognize that you bring much might to our
    fight,
That your powers are at their highest height,
That our battle could last for weeks of days
    and weeks of nights,
That its ferocity will generate much fear and
    fright,
That our clash will occur within full sight
Of all of my children, the black, brown, yellow,
    red, and white
And of all of your wicked band who shall take
    great delight
That Darkness once again challenges Light."

With sarcasm dripping with disrespect and
    disdain,
Swamp Hattie interrupted God, as thunder
    roared and hail rained.

"Forget my band; they're just so many clowns;
They asked me to stop, to avoid a showdown!
They know that when I destroy this globe
Their kingdoms, their powers, their secret
    abodes,
And they, as spirits, all lack the code
To exist in this universe when the Earth
    explodes.

They are traitors, turncoats, one and all!
They will not be at my side when You take
 Your great fall!"

"So be it Swamp Hattie, but, as all Eternity
 attests,
As surely as the oceans are now at their crests,
As certainly as other goblins are to you just
 roach-like pests,
And in spite of the magic, voodoo, and brews
 you vest,
In the end this will be no contest.
You will fail this exam, your final test.
Your challenge will conclude in the end of
 your quest.
Be certain of your challenge! It shall be your
 last request!"

Chapter 7

The War of the Titans

"We shall see
What we shall see!
Now, choose Your weapons for our contest!
Personally, I could care less.
Choose whatever suits You best…
Of Your powers, I am no longer impressed!"

Of her brashness God was not surprised,
Because He now knew and clearly realized
That the fate of the Earth was truly at risk!

Hattie struck first, cloaking the globe in deep
  Darkness.
God countered with great Light that revealed
  the starkness
Of the moon-like landscape Swamp Hattie's
  demolition had carved
Into once fertile deltas where life now
  struggled and people starved.
Like titanic gladiators with the heavens as
  their stage,
God and Swamp Hattie clashed and intensely
  waged
The war to end wars -- a battle that raged!
Each blow dealt more violence than one
  trillion Nagasaki's
And collateral damage that leveled the Rockies

And spawned enormous floods and volcanic
  eruptions galore,
Hideous hurricanes, and so much, much
  more,
Including gargantuan tsunamis from 10.8
  Richter quakes!
It was truly more than the Earth could take!
The Earth began to swell and split at its core --
All as a result of this titanic war
Between Good and Evil at their extremest
  extremes.
The world threatened to burst apart at its
  seams!
The crust cracked and lava spewed forth,
Melting polar caps to the south and north.
The oceans rose quickly engulfing more
  ground,
Swallowing whole cities whose occupants
  drowned.
God seemed impotent as Hattie's plan
  unwound!

Gasping at the results of Swamp Hattie's
  brutality
And cringing at the reality of Mankind's
  mortality,
God countered with measures aimed to

replenish,
But even faster than He could fix and finish,
Swamp Hattie counterattacked and easily
diminished
God's every attempt to block her thrusts.
With His failures He began losing Man's trust,
As Mankind watched their duels from dawn to
dusk.
Her powers were immense;
The situation, intense!

As the battle raged, God realized Earth's end
    was near;
As he pondered this globe's fate, His only
    choices became clear:
Hattie could continue and all life would
    disappear,
Or He could call the Judgment Day and end
    what He held so dear!
But in so doing, Hattie would be destroyed,
Along with all the Evil she employed --
Resulting in her own condemnation
And preventing her contamination
Of other worlds in this universe and beyond
Where intelligence exists but where no man
    has gone.

Chapter 8

God Summons
Hattie's Sailor

Just when it seemed that He had no other
　　choice,
God summoned Hattie's sailor-lover,
　　commanding with His voice:

"You have wandered eternally in search of
　　your love.
I have monitored your quest from high above.
Your diligence in pursuit I have admired,
But you've never found what you desired:
I have protected you from what you now must
　　see.
Brace yourself; you must not flee.
You will not like what you are about to find,
But the fate of all life and of all Mankind
Is now in your hands. You must find a way
To cease the coming of Man's Judgment Day.
You alone possess the singular power
To prevent the arrival of Man's final hour.
I can tell you not what the secret is,
But her clan holds the clue to solve this quiz."

Chapter 9

Hattie and the Sailor Meet Again

Knowing full well he had no option but to
   follow,
The Sailor closed his eyes and tried hard to
   swallow.
He kneeled in front of his almighty God,
Then raised his eyes and gave a nod:

"I am ready, my Lord; I am responsible for
   this.
This is my fate; I accept the risk."
The Sailor bowed his head; God touched his
   soul,
Dispatching him post-haste to find his goal.

"Sailor, you are the last chance for Humanity.
Meet the object of your desire! Meet your dear
   -- Swamp Hattie!"

In a flash, in an instant, the ex-lovers met.
Eye to eye, breath to breath, as close as two
   could possibly get.
What happened next, Heaven shall never
   forget.
All of a sudden Hattie became totally
   distracted,

Confused, bumfuzzled, as her body reacted:
Blood erupted forth from all her pores,
And she vomited viscous, visceral, ungodly
gore.
Her stinking stench began anew;
Now *both* eyes glowed as she continued to
stew.

She breathed fire and brimstone as if from the
  pew
Of a Southern Baptist preacher with tithes well
  past due!
Hattie's emotions exploded
As her memory denoted
How her world had eroded
When her life imploded
Because this lover sailor
Had dared to betray her!
Now his spirit stood and stared in her face
At the very minute she was about to erase
The earth as a planet and the entire human
  race!

Regaining her composure
And sensing a time to bring closure
To the one last episode to which she had
  exposure,
She looked the spirit man right straight in the
  eyes --
He being responsible for her demise.
She forged a mind-lock to avoid any surprise,
Flicked her forked tongue, and began her
  reprise:

"Before I dispatch you, my despicable dear,
Please tell me, pray tell me, I just have to hear:
Just what in Hell are you doing here?!"

The sailor shook violently and tried not to
    puke,
Braced himself firmly and tried not to rebuke
What positively, most certainly could not
    possibly be
His long lost princess, his true love, his one,
    his only…Hattie.
Stunned by the stench and the visual jolt,
His instincts told him quickly to bolt.
The sailor reacted and began to revolt.

Knowing intervention was now or never,
God opened the sailor's skull in order to sever
The connection between what the sailor had
    just seen
And the now fleeting memories of his lovely
    queen.
God's efforts were charmed,
And they completely disarmed
The sailor to the threat of great harm
Posed by this monster called Swamp Hattie.

Hattie's brainwaves boomed out

With scream after scream and shout after
   shout:

"Answer me now! What's this visit about!"

No longer flustered by this shrieking shrew,
The sailor's cortex revealed what God already
   knew:

"I want you to know that I still love you, I do.
Let me into your heart! You must know, too!"

In that instant, Hattie's mind-lock failed!
Her heart opened up and into it he sailed!
He spoke to her heart and she began to flail.
That frigid black organ began to warm!
Hattie fought back hard with hateful thoughts
   that swarmed,
But his presence stirred feelings and
   memories re-formed!
Gathering her wits
And speaking with spits,
She screamed and bellowed
To this sailor fellow:

"What in Hell do you want?
Meld with my mind? No! No! Don't!"

Taking advantage of her lapse
But on the verge of his own collapse,
He gathered his courage to do what he must.
He opened his mind, as Swamp Hattie
  cussed.

"Listen to me! Listen to me! Look in my brain!
There is a story there that you will disdain,
But hear it all now; you absolutely must!
Or God will cremate you; turn you to dust!"

Driven by an instinct long thought extinct,
She probed his cerebrum's secrets as he
  teetered on the brink.
And the story to unfold
Was one to behold!

Here are the facts that the sailor's brain told,
Ones that resolved our mystery now many
  millennia old.

Chapter 10

The Sailor's Story

"I loved you my Hattie; I truly did.
This truth from you has forever been hid.
But now you must hear your deepest down
    fear,
And with my story, my conscience will clear.

I left you not of my own volition,
But under duress from a St. Augustine
    patrician
Who wanted you to be his girl
More than anything in this whole wide world.
That night after I proposed to you,
After I wept with joy knowing we'd say 'We do,'
I went for a walk toward the St. Augustine
    docks
Along the seawall, block after block.
Just as midnight chimed from the cathedral's
    clock,
Four men dressed in black from head to sock
Appeared from nowhere and demanded my
    gold.
When I reached in my pockets to do as told,
They grabbed my arms and clubbed my head.
I collapsed to the ground, almost dead.

When I awoke, I was far out to sea
In the brig of a ship named the *Galilee*

With no chance to escape; no chance to flee.
Shanghaied I was! And I had to agree
To crew on this ship or be tossed in the sea.
As it turned out this was no merchant trader,
But a pirate vessel that sailed the Equator
To pillage and plunder and tear asunder
All ships that blundered either over or under
The latitudes the *Galilee* claimed as her own.
Having no choice, I wore the skull and
   crossbones,

Until one day, with the ugliest of tones,
Our peg-legged Captain took me aside,
Which scared me a lot, I must confide.
He lifted his patch from his bad eye
And placed his hook-hand with the point on
   my thigh.
He stabbed it in deep, trying to make me cry.
The pain was intense; I wanted to die!
He guffawed as I winced; then he took a deep
   sigh.
Removing his hook from the bone in my leg,
He drew a stout ale from his private keg.
Consuming one-half with one single chug,
He belched his orders and handed me his
   mug:

'Drink all that remains in a single slug.
In the bottom you'll find one palmetto bug.
Put it in your mouth and chew it up whole.
Swallow it down. Do as you're told!'

Following his directions, I managed not to
   puke.
I stared back at this maniac, this crazy captain
   kook.
Bellowing between belches that came straight
   from Hell,

He beckoned me to his cabin: 'I have a story
to tell.' "

Chapter 11

The Secret Letter

" 'You have passed my test;
Now you can know the rest.
I tell you this, not at all in jest.
'Twas no accident into my service you were
   pressed.
See this bag of glittering gold?
For its contents you were sold.
Because you handle what I dish out,
Without a whimper, tear, or shout,
You deserve to know and to be told
Why your life and soul were simultaneously
   sold.

A rich politician from St. Augustine's ruling
   class
Had long admired Hattie; he wanted that lass.
The fact that you won her was more than he
   could stand,
And, because he was such a weak and
   corrupted man,
He paid me a king's ransom to follow his plan.
So here you are, far at sea, well away from
   land.
Now, I have worse news yet,
And even I truly regret
What I am about to say.
You remember the other day,

That fast sloop that came our way?
It brought my final payment
For completing your detainment.
It also brought you a private letter,
And even though I should have known better,
I read its contents as a safety measure.
I can assure you, its contents bring no
  pleasure.
You have the right this letter to refuse;
You've earned the honor to freely choose.'

I replied, 'This is so very queer,
Because no one, but no one, knows I am here!'

'One man alone is aware of your plight;
He was responsible for that night.
Now this mayor sends this note,
Sealed with his wax and his family's coat.
It's addressed to you, if you care.
It's yours to read, if you dare.'

He handed me the secret letter,
And, even though I, too, knew better,
I opened it up. I took a deep breath.
I learned then of your death.
I went dumb when I saw your passage;
I went numb when I read your message:

> *'I can't go on; my heart is broken.*
> *My sailor lover left without even a*
>   *token*
> *Or a note to say where or why.*
> *Without my Love, I must die.'*

With your note, my heart broke, too:
No desire to live; nothing more to do.
'Captain,' I asked, 'May I borrow your
   dagger?'
Offering his blade, he turned with no swagger
And swept up the stairs with a stein of his
   lager.
I plunged the steel into my chest,
Piercing my heart and splitting my breast.
The blood gushed forth; I began to stagger.
Death came quickly as I clutched his dagger."

Chapter 12

The Sailor's Search

"My soul ascended seeking salvation,
Seeking the Father of my creation.
Finding admittance through the pearly gates,
My spirit was lifted as I could hardly wait
To see you with your halo and wings
And all those other heavenly things
That one's salvation brings.
Finding you not wherever I looked,
I checked St. Peter's ledger book.
Not seeing your name, I got nervous and
   shook,
Not knowing what course your history took.
After searching Heaven both high and low,
I finally asked St. Peter did he know...
What happened to you? Where did you go?

He said, 'My son, she did not belong here --
Not here, not there, not anywhere.
Don't go looking, for you will never find
The soul of that person who was sweet and
   kind.
Don't go looking, you won't like what you see.
My advice to you: just let it be!'

'I cannot! I cannot! I must search on for now.
There's been a mistake, and, some way, some
   how,

I'll prove to you all she belongs here with me.
Just wait! Just wait! I promise; you'll see!'

I checked out of Heaven at the seventh bell,
Boarded the earth-bound express headed for
  Hell.
Ignoring St. Peter's pleadings that I would not
  like what I found,
I turned in my halo and returned to the
  ground.
Met there by Satan, he ripped off my wings,
Gave me a chain, and attached a neck ring.

Then he handed me a pick and demanded I
  sing,
'Lucifer, my Lucifer, you are my king.
I love you, I love you, for the evil you bring!'

I worked in the ovens of Hell's hottest
  kitchens,
Toiling and boiling without any bitchin',
All the while searching every nook and
  cranny,
And grilling and quizzing every mean kid and
  granny:
Had they known you or seen you or heard
  where you'd be?
But I got the same answer: 'Just stay away
  from me!'
Finally, the Devil caught wind of my search
And faster than Satan could exit a church,
I was cast out of Hell and into Purgatory's
  reach,
And as I left I could hear Lucifer preach:

'I do not want any part of you!
Clearly, you know not with whom you screw!'
Cackling and howling in a most wicked way,
He continued to talk as I ended my stay:
'I hope you find just what you seek.

Because, if you do, you will get a peek
Of what real Hell is and you'll come back to
me!
That is, if you're lucky and get a chance to
flee!'

So I returned to St. Augustine and heard of
your sprees,
But you were gone with the winds; you
disappeared with the breeze.
I searched all the swamps and every haunted
house.
I kept hearing of your terror, the hate in your
blouse.
I sought out the assistance of ghosts, ghouls,
and goblins,
Of witches, sorcerers, warlocks, and
hobnoblins.
But all just said, 'Truly, you must be insane,
To be seeking the source of so much misery
and pain.'

An eternity has come and an eternity has
gone.
I have been sent with one last chance to right
all our wrongs!
You must stop this battle; you must cease this

war.
To this earth you must restore
Peace and tranquility
By ending all hostility.
Follow me and I shall show you the way
To the end our Purgatory and a new day!"

Chapter 13

The Revelation

Hattie's eyes stopped glowing and her smell
   disappeared.
The blood stopped oozing and her skin
   quickly cleared.
"But how can I trust, that after all my evil fun,
I could possibly be forgiven for all that I've
   done?
Heaven won't have me; I am completely dead.
To roaming the earth, I am eternally wed."

"Not true, my Hattie. There is a solution
To end this struggle and revolution,
To end earth's plight and bring resolution
To this terrible ordeal of terrorists' collusion
That led you and your band's mission,
Conducted by you all on your own volitions,
Whose goal was clearly the abolition,
Through terror, warfare, force or fission,
     …of all life on this earth as we currently
     know it.
In fact, dear Hattie, the secrets rest with your
   band --
One of the very ones who developed the plan
To hide your eye and cover your smell,
To make you invisible so no one could tell
Where you were lurking and doing your
   damage;

One who gave you that improbable advantage
That made it impossible for even God to
  manage
The evil that has brought this world to the
  brink.
Which one could it be Hattie? Think hard!
  Think!"

Hattie closed her eyes and established a link
To that day and time when they eliminated her
  stink,
To that hour and moment they doused her
  eye,
To the words and actions that caused so many
  to die.
She thought and thought and searched and
  searched.
Her memory faded! She was left in a lurch.

"Help me, my Sailor! Help me, I say!
I fear I am lost; I have lost the way.
It is now or never; it is my judgment day.
If I only knew how, I would gladly pray!"

"You have seen my mind; you have touched
  my heart.
Trust in my love, and we can have a new

start!"

Hearing these words, Hattie opened her mind;
The sailor stepped in, hoping to find
That clue to salvation for Hattie and all
    mankind.
Studying her memory, frame after frame,
He reviewed every word as each one came.
He analyzed each memory that still remained
For even a hint of a clue that they might
    contain.
Fast-forwarding and reversing at a feverish
    pace,
He studied that day trying to build his case
For the solution to the dilemma that Hattie
    now faced.
He analyzed the voodoo priest and the black
    magic prince...
The thought of eating that datil made his
    whole soul wince.
He eliminated these two and then the
    Seminole witch doctor
Who seemed more a bystander, an observer, a
    proctor.
Focusing finally on the wee warlock wizard,
He found the frame where Hattie grabbed his
    gizzard.

Listening intently to the wizard's words,
He took careful note of what he heard:

"With my family's brew, I'll end your cruel
  hex.
I'll dowse that eye's glow with which you've
  been vexed.
I only have two formulae that I still remember:
The one you want works well in September;
The other only functions in the month of
  December.
Fortunately, Hattie, you have no use for

reclaiming the dead.
So, rather than messing with two, we'll work
  with one instead."

It was the wizard who held the key!
It was the wizard who could end Hattie's spree!
It was the wizard who could set Hattie free!
It was the wizard, whom Hattie detested,
Who knew the secret! That's what her memory
  suggested!

Awakening Swamp Hattie from her trance
With this new knowledge he took a chance
And sent it directly to her thoughts
Which replied immediately with words that
  brought
Great doubt and truly deep dejection
Because of her psyche's total rejection
Of any notion of a resurrection
... led by the wee wimpy warlock wizard.

"Hattie, I beg you, we must take a stance.
We seek our salvation; it's our only chance!
Trust me now; remember our romance.
Summon the wizard; do your mind chants.
Telepathisize your need to all of your clan.
You must do it now! That must be our plan!"

Chapter 14

Hattie Summons the Sorcerers

Succumbing to the pleas of her one-time lover,
Hattie rose toward the stars and began to
  hover.
She transmitted brainwaves in an attempt to
  uncover
The whereabouts of the wizard: below her or
  above her?
Searching all signals for signs of a reply,
She waited patiently; then she began to sigh.
When a cosmic crow came on the fly
And transformed itself right in front of her
  eye
Into a member of her clan…that black magic
  prince guy!

"You called, my Hattie, and I just had to come,
Even though the others think I am dumb,
That only a trap surely awaited me here,
In revenge for our expressing our unmitigated
  fear
And imploring you to end your quest
To rip the earth from north to south and east
  to west.
So tell me now, what do you need?
I will do my best, that is my creed."

"I must see the wizard, that wee warlock man,
The meekest, the mildest, of our band.
I have decided to seek eternal peace,
To ask for salvation, or, at the very least,
To be put to rest in some final way
And to do it now, before the end of this day.
The wizard holds the secret to reclaiming the
    dead--
He has the private formula within his head.
And although I face my future with reluctance
    and dread
To my ultimate fate, I'm ready to be led.
So, to you, as my last request,
Please go and do your very best
To implore upon the wizard and the others,
    too,
To return to me and see what they can do.
My time is up; I shall not renew
My ways of terror. It's now up to you!"

Chapter 15

The End Nears

Extracting sparkly powdery stuff
From a secret pocket in his shirt's French cuff,
The prince sprinkled it about while dancing
   and waving,
Creating a monstrous, feathered, coal-black
   raven
That our princely black magic maven
Saddled and mounted and flew off to their
   haven
That they'd established in the island of Grand
   Cayman,
That hid the wizard, the priest, and the
   Seminole shaman.

Riding his raven into a wave,
The raven and maven dove deep, down, into a
   cave
In the coral cliff that fell into an abyss
That was so well hidden it was easy to
   miss.
Maneuvering his bird through the rising tide
And following the tunnel that twisted inside,
The prince proceeded past rocks and stones,
Giant clam shells and huge piles of whale
   bones.
Finally finding his friends inside a bubble
   dome --

A self-contained palace the renegades called home.

Passing right through its glistening,
  transparent wall,
The prince stopped his steed and called to
  them all:

"My wizard, my shaman, my voodoo priest
  friends,
I come from Swamp Hattie who is at her end.
She has met the spirit of her ex-lover's soul,
The sailor who left her many millennia ago.
Turns out he was shanghaied, torn away from
  his girl.
So he took his own life and left the real world.
He toured both Hell and Heaven above
In search of Hattie, his lost true love!

He has convinced Swamp Hattie that the time
  has now come
To give up her ways and to get away from
The Evil with which she has tortured the earth.
It is time to give up, to seek rebirth.
She needs you…you warlock wizard!
She apologizes profusely for squeezing your
  gizzard.
She believes you and you alone
Can reclaim her soul and let her go home!"

"She is right! She remembers well
That day when you all heard me tell
That I have a secret for reclaiming the Dead,
One of only two brews still intact in my head."

The wizard, priest, and prince turned to the
    shaman
As they stood miles beneath the island of
    Grand Cayman.
The Seminole witch doctor pondered the
    situation;
After all, it was his plan that led to Hattie's
    creation
As a silent terrorist no one could see,
An odorless killer he had set free.
It was he who started this…yes, it was he!

Thinking deep thoughts as he rubbed his gold
    spear,
He studied centuries of memories that he still
    held quite dear.
The static electricity that flashed from his gear
Sparked an idea that brought dread and fear.
But then his instincts made it perfectly clear:

> The end was near;
> *All* their times were here!

Chapter 16

The Seminole
Shaman Speaks

With great solemnity the shaman addressed
   his group,
All together at once, this sorcerers' troop.

"In this chess match we've played for who
   knows how long,
Where we've done our best to do so much
   wrong,
For the last move we no longer must wait:
God has played his hand…it is now
   checkmate!
For you see, we now have no other choice.
We can ignore the pleas of Swamp Hattie's
   voice,
And God will call the Judgment Day.
In His decision, we shall have no say,
As earthquakes and volcanoes do away
With this globe, Swamp Hattie, and spirits like
   us.
This is inevitable; in my words, you can trust.

We also could choose to answer her call,
And, if it's a trick for which we fall,
The outcome is the same: the end of us all.
And, per chance by some mystical quirk,
The wizard's magic magically works,
And we reclaim her soul from the Dead,

Could the wizard's brew not work on us
   instead?
For if it could, maybe, too, our purgatory
   could end.
What do you say, you -- my friends?"

In unison they rose and saluted their leader;
They knew it was time to go and meet her.
God had called, "Checkmate!"
There was no time for debate.
Only time for action and time to discover,
If salvation's secret had come with Hattie's
   sailor lover.

Chapter 17

The Galleon of Death

Knowing that they must get there very fast,
They conjured up a spell which they cast,
And a spirit ship with four full masts
And a skeletonized crew of pirates past

Emerged from the transparent bubble dome
  walls
With a black-bearded captain that belched to
  them all:

"Welcome aboard! Please meet my first mate.
Welcome aboard! Time to meet your final
  fate!"

The Captain roared with laughter
Over jokes of "happily ever after."
Then, like Secretariat's fastest colt,
Like a scared lightning bolt,
Like a shot fired from a gun,
Like an electron on the run,
Like a cosmic monorail,
The Captain set sail --
        For the location of Swamp Hattie!

The Galleon of Death followed Hattie's
  psyche's tractor beams
For only nanoseconds, or so it seemed,
Before it docked at the foot of the once mighty
  queen
Who broke down and sobbed at the sight of
  her team.
Slumped shouldered, slouched, with head

bowed low,
In a trembling voice Hattie spoke to them
   slow:

"I thank you for coming; I can't thank you
   enough.
I apologize for our last meeting when I was so
   gruff.
I apologize, wizard, for playing so rough.
I need your help, wizard, times are tough.
I need the assistance, wizard, of your magic
   potion stuff."

Chapter 18

The Wizard Works

Knowing that Hattie might anticipate the
    worst,
For once, the Seminole witch doctor let the
    wizard speak first.

"We are family, Swamp Hattie, all one clan.
We come, Swamp Hattie, to do what we can
To help you execute your final plan.
We, too, seek to escape from Purgatory's
    eternal grip.
We, too, seek salvation or one last trip
To some final resting place of God's own
    choosing.
We know all will otherwise be lost, so why go
    on losing?

I will do my special brew,
Not just for you,
But for all our sorcerers' crew,
And, for your sailor lover, too.
I will attempt to recall and try to remember
How to reclaim souls from the Dead during
    December.
The formula is complex,
But it's what's needed to breach the hex.
My mind is still groggy,
And more than a little foggy,

From our galleon's galactic glide.
Please give me one second; my brain is sunny-
   side fried!"

Hattie spoke softly, genuinely, without
   pretend:
"Take your time, my wizard friend.
What's a few more seconds when there's an
   eternity to end?"

Knowing at once that Swamp Hattie was
   sincere,
These once evil spirits joined hands and
   gathered near.
A calm and solemnity none had experienced
   in thousands of years
Permeated their souls as they wept with tears!
The Seminole shaman finally broke the
   moment
With an insightful comment that was so
   cogent:

"Wizard, we recognize what is at risk, what is
   at stake.
Do your very, very best to concoct and to
   make
The brew that returns the Dead to Life,

The brew that will end our eternal strife,
The brew of your warlock father and witch
   mother,
The brew known only to you and to no other.
But, if you should not remember
This special brew of December,
We will all understand,
My wee warlock wizard man."

"Amen," echoed the sorcerers, Swamp Hattie,
   and the sailor, too.
When Swamp Hattie mind-locked all of her
   crew,
Each of them felt and each of them knew
That Swamp Hattie found *happiness* in the fact
   that they came.
This fact was the truth; this was no charade
   game.
And these feelings of caring were shared
   among all, as one and the same.
The warmth of the moment burned hearts into
   these beings,
Who looked at each other for the first time
   seeing
          …the emotion of love!
Silently they acknowledged this feeling felt by
   all,

The group turned to the wizard who now
   seemed ten feet tall!

"To have even half a chance,
I must enter a deep, dark trance."

Nodding off, he assumed an odd, arabesque
   stance;
Then he began an outlandish Irish clog dance.
Speaking in tongues from the south of
   France,
His eyes bulged out as he took a sideways
   glance.
He blurted right out, "That's it! That's it! We
   have a chance!
We need a jam jar stuffed with one thousand
   lightning bugs.
We need one thousand miniature dancers
   caged in earthen jugs.
We each need identical ancient prayer rugs.
We need a campfire made of first growth
   Celtic wood;
It needs to burn hot; it needs to burn good.
We will spread out the rugs to encircle the
   flames,
Kneel down on the ground, and recite our
   names.

When the fire's flames reach forty feet high
And the smoke is thick, black, and blots out
   the sky,
I'll recite a Celtic rhyme and then free the little
   dancers
Who will interact with our fireflies to give us
   our answers!"

Chapter 19

The Wizard Fails!

Using their powerful magic for probably the
  last time,
The sorcerers and Hattie, as in their prime,
Procured what they needed…including the
  Celtic rhyme!

They stoked the fire first, and it lit up the
  night.
It burned really hot, and it burned really
  bright.
As the flames reached fully forty feet high,
They positioned their rugs and wondered how
  and why
One thousand fairy dancers and one thousand
  glowing ants
Could ever give the answer, even with the wee
  wizard's rants!
The ebony black smoke soon cloaked the
  heavenly lights,
So the wizard assumed his position, then
  chanted with all his might:

"Edded…medded…preved…undeaded;
Saidded…credded…non-unwedded."

On his last syllable the jar and jugs dissolved
  away,

Releasing the bugs and fairies to come out and
  play.
Each tiny dancer saddled its favorite firefly
And rode it up…up…up and away, into the
  midnight sky.

Sparking off their glow bulbs, the bugs formed
one long straight line
That began to oscillate, wiggle, round up, and
combine
To form chemiluminescent words that
appeared one after another…one at a time!

Our sorcerers' troop and sailor read each word
aloud,
As each one glowed chartreuse against the
dark, smoky clouds:

"There…..is…..no…..magic…..potion…..
chant…..or…..spell…..
That…..can…..reclaim…..one…..from…..
the…..Dead…..or…..remove…..one…..
from….
…..Hell!"

Chapter 20

Swamp Hattie
or *Hattie ?*

All gasped in unison when the meaning sank
  in.
The Seminole shaman sat stunned; he knew
  not where to begin.
The voodoo priest and black magic prince
Sent mind-waves to all: "This makes no
  sense!"
The poor warlock wizard dropped down on
  one knee,
Bowed his head, and offered his plea:

"My mother's magic and my father's spells!
  How could they desert wee little me??
I have failed each of you, my friends, and,
  especially… my Swamp Hattie."

Turning to Hattie, all feared what she would
  do,
But, in the same moment, the sailor looked
  into her eyes and instantly knew
That Swamp Hattie was gone…and *his* Hattie
  renewed!

Taking Hattie's hands, he held them to his
  chest;
Hattie then laid her head onto his left breast!

The sailor guy kissed this being through her
   mossy gray hair,
An event so miraculous the sorcerers just had
   to stare!
Hattie raised her head high; her eyes flowed
   with tears!
She spoke softly and slowly to ease their fears:
"It matters not, my shaman, my priest, my
   prince, and my wee little friend.
We've all done our best to change, and, in the
   end,
The very fact that you came means the world
   to me.
And I now have my sailor, as you can plainly
   see.
So, even if we must wander for the rest of
   eternity,
We will all go together with the certainty
That we have each other,
And I think we have uncovered
That we have a love for one another,
Like father and son, like sister and brother,
That will ease our fateful story
And our journey through Purgatory."

In one last gesture to seal their private pact,
Hattie discarded her beaded bracelet in a final
   act
To signify that she would never retract...
         Her vows of this moment!

The sorcerers, the sailor, and Hattie joined in
   embrace --
Intellectually at first, then in spirit and body...
   arm in arm and face to face!

Chapter 21

God Appears

During that moment of deep introspection,
The band was helpless, without protection,
And so completely overwhelmed by the
    feelings of affection
That none of them noticed that the smoke had
    cleared
And that God Himself had silently appeared…
                    …right in their very midst!

"You each now know that there is no mystical
    cure
For what you have wrought and what you have
    endured.
There is no magical chant or special spell
That can reclaim one from the Dead or
    remove one from Hell.
Salvation is not found in any potion or brew.
Rather, it's found by what you feel in your
    heart and by what you do.
You have found the Answer; nothing could
    please me more.
So now I can reclaim you from the Dead, and
    then I shall be free to restore
Your souls to be among the Living…
Your rewards for loving, caring, and giving!
So, prepare yourselves to re-enter the other
    side

For the first time since each of you originally
   died!"

To make certain each had repented from their
   crimes,
God addressed them each, one at a time.
Finding not one single, solitary regret,
God prepared them for what they were about
   to get;
God prepared them for the fate He'd set:

     Using nuclear fission to restore the norm,
     God split each sorcerer into two forms.
     The evil parts He cauterized and poured
       them down a well,
     Where Lucifer met them at the bottom
       and welcomed them to Hell.
     The salvaged souls He forgave and fitted
       them with wings.
     He flew them off to Heaven, where His
       angels sing.

God then turned to the lover pair,
Whom He handled with great care.
"Your Purgatory will expire.
It's time for the events to transpire."

Following His command, Hattie and the
  Sailor kneeled
And bowed their heads as their fates were
  sealed.
Unleashing the Power that built the
  universe,
God threw time and reality into reverse.
When this holy time machine reached the
  perfect place and date,
God reached out His hand to extract the
  Good and separate…
    …the Bad.
God removed Hattie's beacon eye and
  returned it to her lair:
A clear warning to others to never, ever go
  there!
He bottled up her stinking stench and
  spread it everywhere.
He pulverized Hattie's wicked parts,
  strewing them around the sphere.
He took the sailor's few bad pieces,
  spreading them far and near.
Then the guy sailor's Good spirit and the
  girl's
Rose and whirled in an accelerating swirl
And became what they were millennia
  ago:

Beautiful young lovers with Heaven in tow.
As quickly as they formed, they rocketed
  from sight
At warp speed times a thousand, they
  streaked through the night
To the far reaches of our universe: two
  angels' maiden flights

That ended with an implosion, a
   supernova flash,
A gamma ray burst, a thunderous
   crash --
A thermonuclear event in a galaxy far
   away
With the death of a legend on an eternally
   fateful day.
And the birth of a brilliant, dayglo blue
   star
As the power of love shown from afar.
A star that shone all 'round the earth
That showed the Way to new birth;
A star that still shines to this very day;
A star that continues to light the Way!

There could be no doubt-- the victory was His!
Beings euthanized by God Almighty in answer
   to the quiz:
The power of Good versus the power of Bad;
The feelings of Happy versus the feelings of
   Sad;
The trait of Greed versus the trait of Giving;
The act of Dying versus the act of Living;
The emotion of Love versus the emotion of
   Hate.
He showed them all that it's never too late!

Epilogue

God reclaimed these souls from the side of
the Dark,
And, in receiving the two lovers, He made
these remarks:

"The world has its evils, bad people, and
ghosts,
But the ones that are the greatest threats, the
ones I fear the most,
Are those who own avarice, vanity and hate;
Those who care not for others and who
cannot wait
To look in the mirror and admire what they
see;
Those who hoard all their money and ignore
others' pleas
To help those less fortunate, those in deep
need.
So now, my Hattie, your legend's complete.
It will live forever; all will repeat
Your story of evil and your final defeat.
With this ultimate message it will be replete:

It's never too late to change one's ways.
Everyone has until one's Judgment Day.
The love of one person can change the
world,

Be that person man, woman, boy, or girl.
And the power of God shall always
    overcome.

Welcome to my kingdom, Hattie!
Your kingdom is won!"

The End

Book 3

For Swamp Hattie news,
updates, and more...

Visit
SwampHattie.com

Dennis M. Smith Jr.
"Hattie's Daddy"

About the Author

"Hattie's Daddy" has been a self-proclaimed "closet poet" since his 7th grade English teacher encouraged his secret interest. As a board-certified anatomic and clinical pathologist and transfusion medicine specialist, he has written or edited many scientific and medical articles, chapters, and texts. However, *The Legend of Swamp Hattie* is his first fictional effort. Recently, the author has sold several fishing articles to a major outdoor magazine. He is also participating in a joint project with world-renown artist Dean Mitchell which will pair Mitchell's paintings with the author's poetry.

A true believer in the power of education, Hattie's Daddy serves on the Committee of Visitors for Vanderbilt University's School of Engineering, the Board of Directors of Jacksonville Country Day School, and the faculty of the Young Writers' Workshop in Jacksonville.

Stay tuned! More Swamp Hattie adventures are on the way. To learn more about what the future.. or past... holds, visit SwampHattie.com …just be careful where you go after dark!

Dennis M. Smith Jr.

About the Artist

"Once, when doing a radio interview, I was asked when I first decided that I was destined to be an artist. My reply was 'When I realized that I could color between the lines in my coloring book.' As a graduate of Ringling School of Art, I have never done anything other than illustrate: stories, articles, books, magazines, newspapers and the occasional work for advertising agencies. My career began at Hallmark Cards in Kansas City, MO, followed by positions as a newspaper illustrator. I opened Smackwater Studio, Inc., in 1986, starting with work as a wildlife illustrator, which led to work for almost every outdoor publication and publisher in the U.S. When Dennis approached me about doing the art for *Swamp Hattie*, I was inspired by his poetry. I believe we matched our ideas and produced spell-binding books that will not be soon forgotten. I'm very proud to be a part of this project and am having more fun than the law allows in producing illustrations for these amazing books."

Chris Armstrong
SmackWaterStudio.com

Other Books by Dennis M. Smith Jr.

The Trilogy of Swamp Hattie
The Collector's Edition
Hardcover, 8.5" x 11," full color, illustrated with
over 75 incredible, original works of art created
specifically for the book!

Coming Soon...

The Mystery of the Mill Creek Mud Monster
A good guardian monster, an evil phantom wolf, a
lost little girl: Chance casts them together—
can fate and faith cast out the bad?

The Witches of Cattle Creek Crossing
Ravaged by swamp-water fever, old St. Augustine's
children mysteriously disappear,
and the town's citizens seek revenge and retribu-
tion on six swamp witch sisters!

Coming later...
the Swamp Hattie saga continues...

The Daughter of Swamp Hattie
Before being expelled from Hell, Swamp Hattie
gives birth to the Devil's only child, a beautiful
daughter who possesses the most evil genes and
powers in the existence of the earth! The Devil
concocts a plan and sends his 13-year-old daughter
to the surface to lay the foundation for the Devil's
ultimate triumph and the world's darkest hour!

What people are saying about *Swamp Hattie*

"...extremely well-written and inventive- most people do not have the patience or the talent to craft poetry- and, to top it off, the artwork is beautiful!"

- E.K., editor, New York, New York

"...incredible story, poetry, and art...the end of the trilogy is especially well-done, inspiring, and uplifting...you have been blessed with a special talent..."

- Joseph Clayton, Founding Principal and President, Briarcrest Christian School, and Member, Shelby County School Board, Memphis, Tennessee

"...unbelievably good...I couldn't put it down...what's next?!!!!"

- Lana Bourdon, career educator and kindergarten teacher, retired, Jacksonville, Florida

"I have read several of Dennis' fishing articles; they are witty, entertaining, informative, and, occasionally, even a bit grotesque in a comical way. But Swamp Hattie elevates things to an entirely different level: awesome plot, characters, and art! This manuscript reads so well and so easily…it should definitely be published!"

- Michael Pellini, M.D., physician, corporate executive, and entrepreneur, Dana Point, CA

"I love fantasy and this is as good as it gets! When can I find out what happens next?"

- Kapila Ratnam, Ph.D., Biochemistry, Investment Professional, Philadelphia, Pennsylvania

"What a read! Striking imagery…I was captivated from the first line. I even stole the second volume from my colleague's desk so I could read it before her. I don't usually read fantasy, but this manuscript is outstanding. Can't wait to see the artwork for the second two portions of the trilogy!"

- Brian Murphy, Managing Director, Newspring Capital, King of Prussia, PA

What kids are saying about *Swamp Hattie*

From Mrs. Miniard and her 7th grade students

"Dennis is an amazing writer. I read the first page to my 7th grade class and they remained spellbound until the very last sentence! Love never fails…"

- Holley Miniard, 7th grade teacher,
Ponte Vedra Beach, Florida

…and her students:

"…she (Swamp Hattie) is really creepy…great for my age…you should sell it in stores because it will be a big hit!"

"…really liked it! If it was in our library, I'd check it out. Would you give a copy to our library?"

…and our favorite…

"…I loved your story and the ryming [sic]. It is not scary at all. Sorry, but it was just disgusting. If you want something scary, write about middle school boys…
THAT'S SCARY!"